Disney's Aladdin

Adapted by Karen Kreider
Illustrated by Darrell Baker

 A GOLDEN BOOK • NEW YORK

Copyright © 1992, 2004 Disney Enterprises, Inc. All rights reserved under International and Pan-American Copyright Conventions. Published in the United States by Golden Books, an imprint of Random House Children's Books, a division of Random House, Inc., New York, and simultaneously in Canada by Random House of Canada Limited, Toronto, in conjunction with Disney Enterprises, Inc. Originally published by Golden Books in 1992. Golden Books, A Golden Book, A Little Golden Book, the G colophon, and the distinctive gold spine are registered trademarks of Random House, Inc.

Library of Congress Control Number: 2003109743

ISBN: 0-7364-2259-5

www.randomhouse.com/kids/disney

www.goldenbooks.com

First Random House Edition 2004

Printed in the United States of America   10 9 8 7 6

One night, an evil man named Jafar and his wicked parrot, Iago, were waiting in a faraway desert.

Soon a thief named Gazeem rode up to them and held out the missing half of a scarab medallion. When Jafar fit the halves together, lightning flashed and the medallion raced across the sand.

Jafar and the thief followed the medallion to the Cave of Wonders. Jafar ordered Gazeem to get the magic lamp that was hidden inside. But when the thief entered, he was eaten by the tiger head entrance!

Then the tiger head spoke: "Only one who is worthy may enter here!"

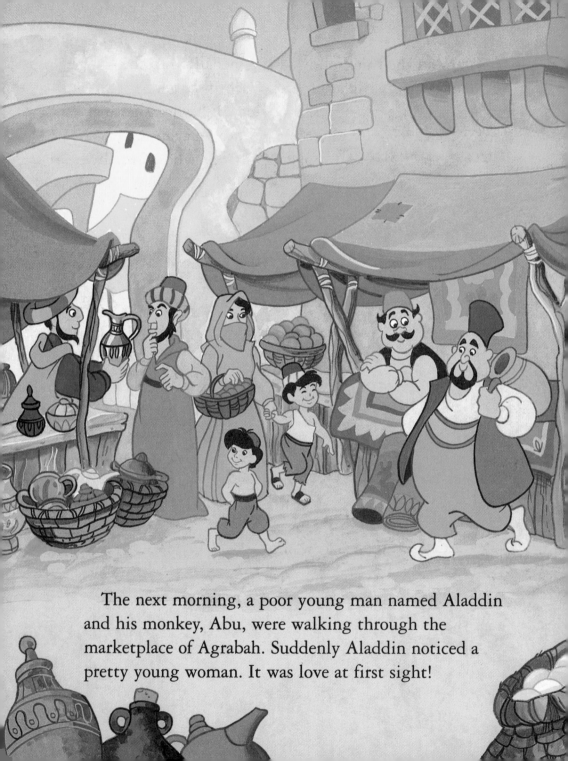

The next morning, a poor young man named Aladdin
and his monkey, Abu, were walking through the
marketplace of Agrabah. Suddenly Aladdin noticed a
pretty young woman. It was love at first sight!

The young woman took an apple from a fruit seller's cart to give to a hungry boy. When the man demanded payment, which she did not have, Aladdin and Abu rushed to help her.

"Thank you for finding my sister," Aladdin said to the fruit seller. He quickly led the young woman away.

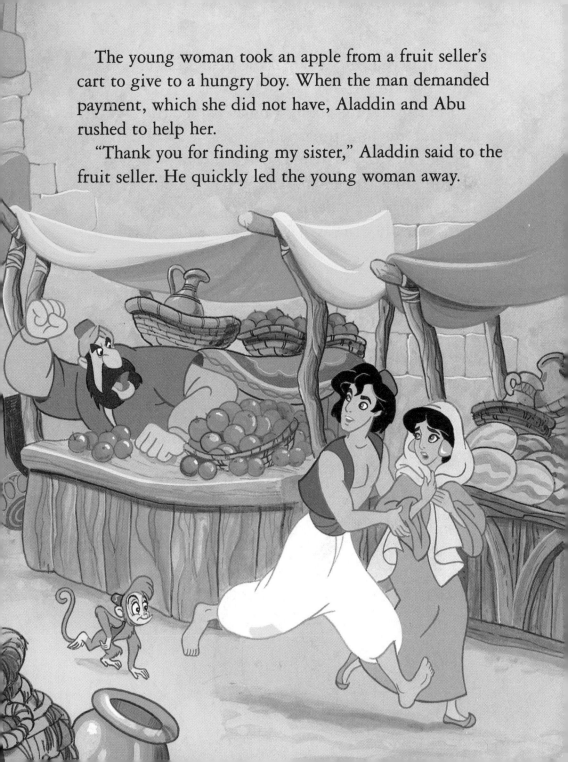

"This is your first time in the marketplace, huh?" asked Aladdin.

"I ran away," the young woman explained. "My father is forcing me to get married."

Suddenly, palace guards appeared. They arrested Aladdin under orders from Jafar, the Sultan's advisor. The young woman demanded that they release him. She was really Princess Jasmine, the Sultan's daughter!

Princess Jasmine returned to the palace and ordered
Jafar to release Aladdin. Jafar told her it was too late—
the young man had been killed.

But Aladdin was not dead. Jafar had learned that
Aladdin was the only person worthy to enter the Cave of
Wonders. Aladdin could bring the magic lamp to Jafar!

Jafar took Aladdin to the Cave of Wonders. "Proceed," said the tiger head. "Touch nothing but the lamp."

Aladdin and Abu gasped when they saw all the gold and jewels in the cavern. They even found a Magic Carpet!

But just as Aladdin spotted the magic lamp, Abu touched a huge, glittering jewel.

With a loud rumble, the cave began to collapse. Aladdin and Abu were trapped!

But Abu still had the magic lamp!
Aladdin took the old lamp and tried to rub off some of the dust.
Poof! In a flash of swirling smoke, a gigantic genie appeared.
"You're a lot smaller than my last master," he said to Aladdin.

The Genie whisked them all out of the cave on the Magic Carpet. Then he told Aladdin that he had three wishes.

Aladdin asked the Genie what *he* would wish for.

The Genie replied, "I would wish for freedom!"

So Aladdin promised to use his third wish to set the Genie free. But his *first* wish was to be a prince—so that he could marry Princess Jasmine.

Meanwhile, at the palace, Jafar used his serpent staff to hypnotize the Sultan. The poor Sultan was about to agree that Jafar could marry Jasmine.

Suddenly they heard the sounds of a parade. The spell was broken. The Sultan rushed to the balcony in time to see the arrival of a grand prince. It was Aladdin!

Aladdin entered the throne room.

"Your Majesty," he said, bowing to the Sultan. "I am Prince Ali Ababwa. I have come to seek your daughter's hand in marriage."

The Sultan was thrilled! The law stated that Jasmine must marry a prince before her next birthday—which was only days away.

But the princess did not want to marry Prince Ali. She was not in love with him.

Prince Ali offered the princess a ride on his Magic
Carpet, hoping to win her love.

During the magical journey, Princess Jasmine
realized that Prince Ali was the young man who had
helped her in the marketplace. That starry night,
Aladdin and Princess Jasmine fell in love.

Jafar didn't want anyone else to marry Jasmine and foil his evil plans. He was so angry that he had Prince Ali captured and thrown into the sea.

Luckily, Aladdin had the magic lamp with him. He summoned the Genie and asked for his second wish— to save his life! The Genie quickly transported Aladdin back to the palace in Agrabah.

Jafar was determined to marry Princess Jasmine.

"I will never marry you, Jafar!" cried Jasmine. "I choose Prince Ali!"

But the Sultan was under Jafar's spell, and he ordered his daughter to marry Jafar.

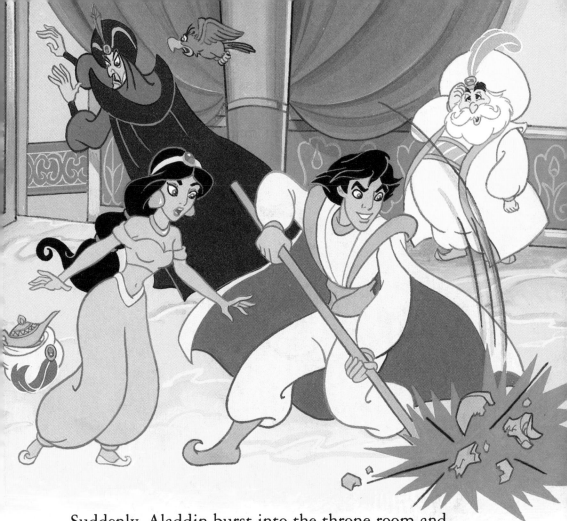

Suddenly, Aladdin burst into the throne room and smashed Jafar's serpent staff.

"He's been controlling you with this, Your Highness!" said Aladdin.

Immediately, the spell was broken.

"Traitor!" shouted the Sultan. "Guards, arrest Jafar!"

But before they could capture him, Jafar escaped to his secret laboratory.

As Jafar fled, he noticed that Prince Ali was carrying the magic lamp. The prince was really Aladdin! Jafar ordered his parrot to steal the lamp.

When Iago returned, Jafar made the Genie appear. "I wish to be Sultan!" he demanded.

The moment had come for the Sultan to announce the
wedding of Princess Jasmine and Prince Ali Ababwa.
A cheering crowd had gathered in front of the palace.

Suddenly Jafar appeared—in the Sultan's robes!
The crowd gasped.

"Genie, what have you done?" Aladdin shouted.

"Sorry, kid," said the Genie sadly. "I've got a new
master now."

Then Jafar made his second wish—to be the most powerful sorcerer in the world. Jafar the sorcerer lost no time turning Prince Ali back into Aladdin.

"Jasmine, I'm sorry!" cried Aladdin. "I'm not a prince. I can't marry you."

Finally Jafar banished Aladdin to the ends of the earth. When Aladdin found himself a million miles from nowhere, he was glad that Abu and the Magic Carpet were still with him. "Back to Agrabah!" he shouted to the Carpet. "As fast as you can!"

Jafar was in the throne room, enjoying his newfound power, when Aladdin appeared. "How many times do I have to destroy you, boy?" he roared.

"You cowardly snake!" Aladdin shouted.

"Snake?" snarled Jafar. With a loud hiss, he turned himself into a giant cobra.

Looking up at the power-hungry Jafar, Aladdin got an idea. "The Genie has more power than you'll ever have!" he jeered.

"Yes-s-s-s," hissed Jafar. "You're right. I'm ready to make my third wish. I wish to be a genie."

The moment Jafar turned into a genie, Aladdin smiled. Jafar had forgotten that a genie must live in a lamp. In an instant, he and Iago disappeared inside their own magic lamp. They were gone for good!

The Sultan was overjoyed. That very day he changed
the law so that Jasmine could marry any man she chose.
And she chose Aladdin!

And what did Aladdin do with his third wish? He
kept his promise and wished for the Genie's freedom.

"Look out, world!" exclaimed the Genie. "Here I
come. I'm free!"